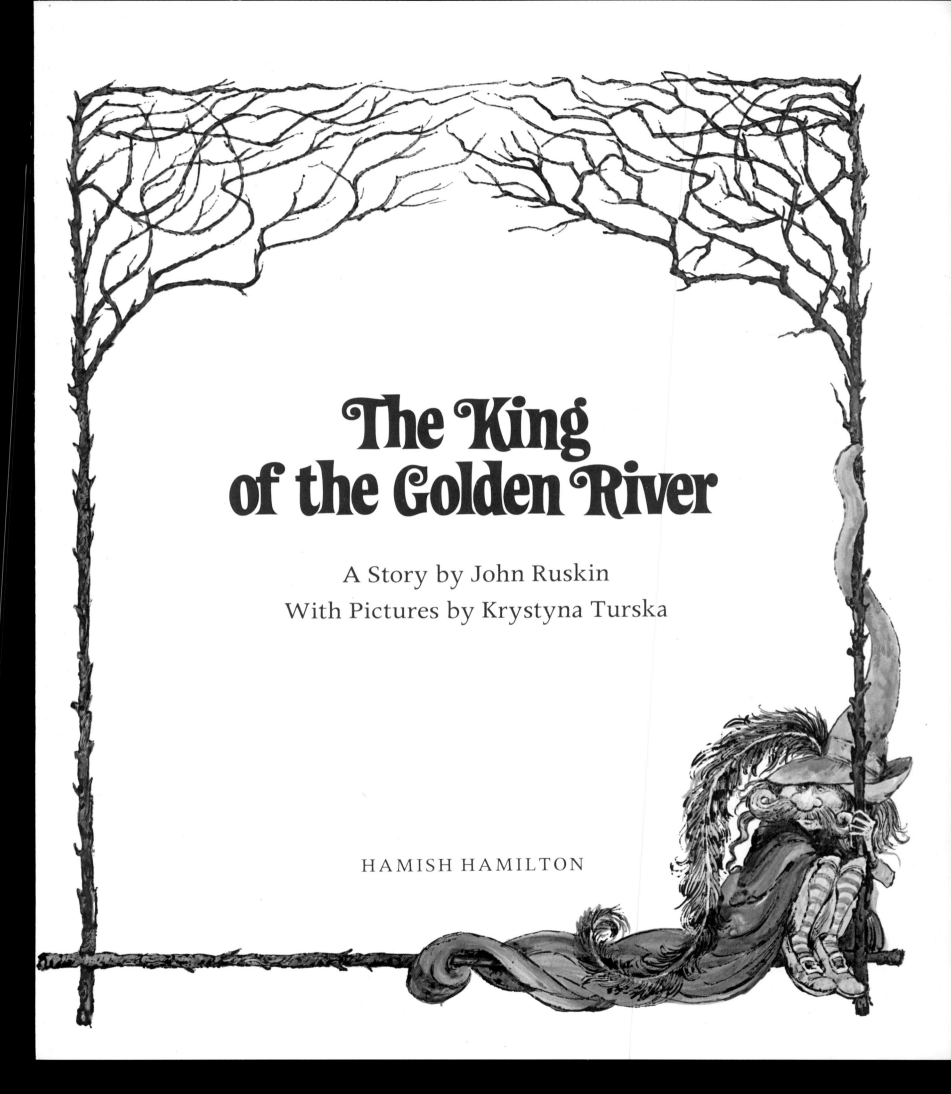

The King
of the Golden River

A Story by John Ruskin

With Pictures by Krystyna Turska

HAMISH HAMILTON

12. 2. 1978

Thank you for introducing me
to the King.

Krystyna Turska.

For Julia, with love
K.T.

Illustrations © 1978 Krystyna Turska
First published in Great Britain 1978 by
Hamish Hamilton Children's Books Ltd,
90 Great Russell Street, London WC1B 3PT
ISBN 0 241 89554 5
Printed in Great Britain by
Cox & Wyman Ltd, London, Fakenham and Reading

In a secluded and mountainous part of Stiria, there was, in old time, a valley of the most surprising and luxuriant fertility. It was surrounded, on all sides, by steep and rocky mountains, rising into peaks, which were always covered with snow, and from which a number of torrents descended in constant cataracts. One of these fell westward, over the face of a crag so high, that, when the sun had set to everything else, and all below was darkness, his beams still shone full upon this waterfall, so that it looked like a shower of gold. It was, therefore, called by the people of the neighbourhood, the Golden River.

It was strange that none of these streams fell into the valley itself. They all descended on the other side of the mountains, and wound away through broad plains and by populous cities. But the clouds were drawn so constantly to the snowy hills, and rested so softly in the circular hollow, that in time of drought and heat, when all the country round was burnt up, there was still rain in the little valley; and its crops were so heavy, and its hay so high, and its apples so red, and its grapes so blue, and its wine so rich, and its honey so sweet, that it was a marvel to everyone who beheld it, and was commonly called the Treasure Valley.

The whole of this little valley belonged to three brothers, called Schwartz, Hans and Gluck. Schwartz and Hans, the two elder brothers, were very ugly men, with overhanging eyebrows and small dull eyes, which were always half shut, so that you couldn't see into *them*, and always fancied they saw very far into *you*.

They lived by farming the Treasure Valley, and very good farmers they were. They killed everything that did not pay for its eating. They shot the blackbirds, because they pecked the fruit; and killed the hedgehogs, lest they should suck the cows; they poisoned the crickets for eating the crumbs in the kitchen, and smothered the cicadas, which used to sing all summer in the lime-trees. They worked their servants without any wages, till they would not work any more, and then quarrelled with them, and turned them out of doors without paying them.

It would have been very odd, if with such a farm, and such a system of farming, they hadn't got very rich; and very rich they *did* get. They generally contrived to keep their corn by them till it was very dear, and then sell it for twice its value; they had heaps of gold lying about on their floors, yet it was never known that they had given so much as a penny or a crust to charity; they never went to mass; grumbled perpetually at paying tithes; and were, in a word, of so cruel and grinding a temper, as to receive from all those with whom they had any dealings, the nickname of the 'Black Brothers'.

The youngest brother, Gluck, was as completely opposed, in both appearance and character, to his seniors as could possibly be imagined or desired. He was not above twelve years old, fair, blue-eyed, and kind in temper to every living thing. He did not, of course, agree particularly well with his brothers, or rather, they did not agree with *him*. He was usually appointed to the honourable office of turnspit, when there was anything to roast, which was not often; for, to do the brothers justice, they were hardly less sparing upon themselves than upon other people. At other times he used to clean the shoes, floors, and sometimes the plates, occasionally getting what was left on them, by way of encouragement, and a wholesome quantity of dry blows, by way of education.

Things went on in this manner for a long time. At last came a very wet summer, and everything went wrong in the country round. The hay had hardly been got in, when the haystacks were floated bodily down to the sea by an inundation; the vines were cut to pieces with the hail; the corn was all killed by a black blight; only in the Treasure Valley, as usual, all was safe. As it had rain when there was rain nowhere else, so it had sun when there was sun nowhere else. Everybody came to buy corn at the farm, and went away pouring maledictions on the Black Brothers. They asked what they liked, and got it, except from the poor people, who could only beg, and several of whom were starved at their very door without the slightest regard or notice.

It was drawing towards winter, and very cold weather, when one day the two elder brothers had gone out, with their usual warning to little Gluck, who was left to mind the roast, that he was to let nobody in, and give nothing out. Gluck sat down quite close to the fire, for it was raining very hard, and the kitchen walls were by no means dry or comfortable looking. He turned and turned, and the roast got nice and brown. "What a pity," thought Gluck, "my brothers never ask anybody to dinner. I'm sure, when they've got such a nice piece of mutton as this, and nobody else has got so much as a piece of dry bread, it would do their hearts good to have somebody to eat it with them."

Just as he spoke, there came a double knock at the house door, yet heavy and dull, as though the knocker had been tied up—more like a puff than a knock. "It must be the wind," said Gluck; "nobody else would venture to knock double knocks at our door." No, it wasn't the wind: there it came again very hard, and what was particularly astounding, the knocker seemed to be in a hurry, and not to be in the least afraid of the consequences.

Gluck went to the window, opened it, and put his head out to see who it was. It was the most extraordinary-looking little gentleman he had ever seen in his life. He had a very long nose, slightly brass-coloured, and expanding towards its termination into a development not unlike the lower extremity of a key bugle. His cheeks were very round, and very red, and might have warranted a

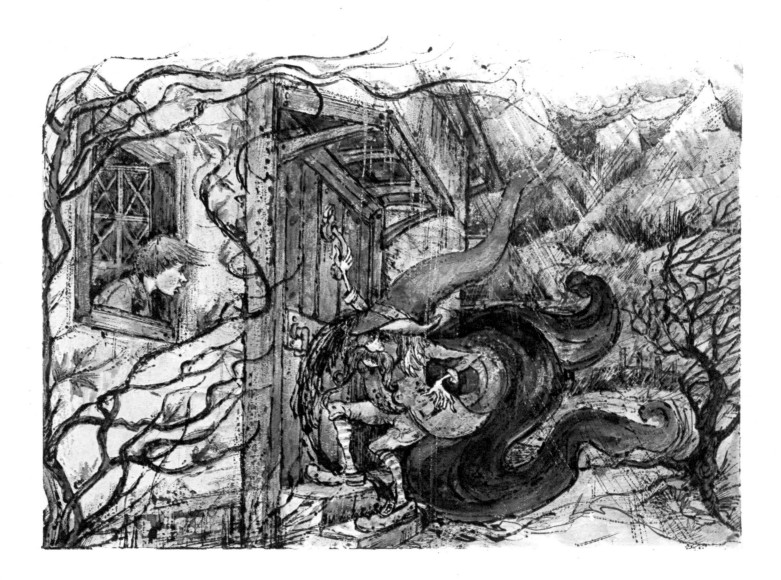

supposition that he had been blowing a refractory fire for the last eight-and-forty hours. His eyes twinkled merrily through long silky eyelashes, his moustaches curled twice round like a corkscrew on each side of his mouth, and his hair, of a curious mixed pepper-and-salt colour, descended far over his shoulders.

He was about four feet six in height, and wore a conical pointed cap of nearly the same altitude, decorated with a black feather some three feet long. His doublet was prolonged behind into something resembling a violent exaggeration of what is now termed a 'swallow tail', but was much obscured by the swelling folds of an enormous, glossy-looking cloak, which must have been very much too long in calm weather, as the wind, whistling round the old house, carried it clear out from the wearer's shoulders to about four times his own length.

Gluck was so perfectly paralysed by the singular appearance of his visitor, that he remained fixed without uttering a word, until the old gentleman, having performed another, and a more energetic concerto on the knocker, turned round to look after his fly-away cloak. In so doing he caught sight of Gluck's little yellow head jammed in the window, with his mouth and eyes very wide open indeed.

''Hallo!'' said the little gentleman, ''that's not the way to answer the door: I'm wet, let me in.''

To do the little gentleman justice, he *was* wet. His feather hung down between his legs like a beaten puppy's tail, dripping like an umbrella; and from the ends of his moustaches the water was running into his waistcoat pockets, and out again like a mill-stream.

''I beg pardon, sir,'' said Gluck, ''I'm very sorry, but I really can't.''

''Can't what?'' said the old gentleman.

''I can't let you in, sir—I can't indeed; my brothers would beat me to death, sir, if I thought of such a thing. What do you want, sir?''

''Want?'' said the old gentleman petulantly. ''I want fire, and shelter; and there's your great fire there blazing, crackling, and dancing on the walls, with nobody to feel it. Let me in, I say; I only want to warm myself.''

Gluck had had his head, by this time, so long out of the window that he began to feel it was really unpleasantly cold, and when he turned and saw the beautiful fire rustling and roaring and throwing long bright tongues up the chimney, as if it were licking its chops at the savoury smell of the leg of mutton, his heart melted within him that it should be burned away for nothing. "He does look *very* wet," said little Gluck; "I'll just let him in for a quarter of an hour." Round he went to the door and opened it; and as the little gentleman walked in, there came a gust of wind through the house that made the chimney totter.

"That's a good boy," said the little gentleman. "Never mind your brothers. I'll talk to them."

"Pray, sir, don't do any such thing," said Gluck. "I can't let you stay till they come; they'd be the death of me."

"Dear me," said the old gentleman, "I'm very sorry to hear that. How long may I stay?"

"Only till the mutton's done, sir," replied Gluck, "and it's very brown."

Then the old gentleman walked into the kitchen, and sat himself down on the hob, with the top of his cap accommodated up the chimney, for it was a great deal too high for the roof.

"You'll soon dry there, sir," said Gluck, and sat down again to turn the mutton. But the old gentleman did *not* dry there, but went on drip, drip, dripping among the cinders, and the fire fizzed, and sputtered, and began to look very black, and uncomfortable; never was such a cloak; every fold in it ran like a gutter.

"I beg pardon, sir," said Gluck at length, after watching the water spreading in long, quicksilver-like streams over the floor for a quarter of an hour; "Mayn't I take your cloak?"

"No, thank you," said the old gentleman.

"Your cap, sir?"

"I am all right, thank you," said the old gentleman rather gruffly.

"But—sir—I'm very sorry," said Gluck, hesitatingly; "but—really, sir—you're—putting the fire out."

"It'll take longer to do the mutton then," replied his visitor dryly.

Gluck was very much puzzled by the behaviour of his guest; it was such a strange mixture of coolness and humility. He turned away at the string meditatively for another five minutes.

"That mutton looks very nice," said the old gentleman at length. "Can't you give me a little bit?"

"Impossible, sir," said Gluck.

"I'm very hungry," continued the old gentleman. "I've had nothing to eat yesterday, nor today. They surely couldn't miss a bit from the knuckle!"

He spoke in so very melancholy a tone that it quite melted Gluck's heart. "They promised me one slice today, sir," said he. "I can give you that, but not a bit more."

"That's a good boy," said the old gentleman again.

Then Gluck warmed a plate, and sharpened a knife. "I don't care if I do get beaten for it," thought he. Just as he had cut a large slice out of the mutton, there came a tremendous rap at the door. The old gentleman jumped off the hob, as if it had suddenly become inconveniently warm. Gluck fitted the slice into the mutton again, with desperate efforts at exactitude, and ran to open the door.

"What did you keep us waiting in the rain for?" said Schwartz, as he walked in, throwing his umbrella in Gluck's face. "Ay! what for, indeed, you little vagabond?" said Hans, administering an education box on the ear, as he followed his brother into the kitchen.

"Bless my soul!" said Schwartz, when he opened the door.

"Amen," said the little gentleman, who had taken his cap off, and was standing in the middle of the kitchen, bowing with the utmost possible velocity.

"Who's that?" said Schwartz, catching up a rolling-pin and turning to Gluck with a fierce frown.

"I don't know, indeed, brother," said Gluck in great terror.

"How did he get in?" roared Schwartz.

"My dear brother," said Gluck deprecatingly, "he was so *very* wet!"

The rolling-pin was descending on Gluck's head; but, at the instant, the old gentleman interposed his conical cap, on which it crashed with a shock that shook the water out of it all over the room. What was very odd, the rolling-pin no sooner touched the cap than it flew out of Schwartz's hand, spinning like a straw in a high wind, and fell into the corner at the farther end of the room.

"Who are you, sir?" demanded Schwartz, turning upon him.

"What's your business?" snarled Hans.

"I'm a poor old man, sir," the little gentleman began very modestly, "and I saw your fire through the window, and begged shelter for a quarter of an hour."

"Have the goodness to walk out again, then," said Schwartz. "We've quite enough water in our house, without making it a drying-house."

"It is a cold day to turn an old man out in, sir; look at my grey hairs." They hung down to his shoulders, as I told you before.

"Ay!" said Hans, "there are enough of them to keep you warm. Walk!"

"I'm very, very hungry, sir; couldn't you spare me a bit of bread before I go?"

"Bread, indeed!" said Schwartz; "do you suppose we've nothing to do with our bread but to give it to such red-nosed fellows as you?"

"Why don't you sell your feather?" said Hans, sneeringly. "Out with you."

"A little bit," said the old gentleman.

"Be off!" said Schwartz.

"Pray, gentlemen."

"Off, and be hanged!" cried Hans, seizing him by the collar. But he had no sooner touched the old gentleman's collar than away he went after the rolling-pin, spinning round and round, till he fell into the corner on the top of it. Then Schwartz was very angry, and ran at the old gentleman to turn him out; but he also had hardly touched him, when away he went after Hans and the rolling-pin, and hit his head against the wall as he tumbled into the corner. And so there they lay, all three.

Then the old gentleman spun himself round with velocity in the opposite direction; continued to spin until his long cloak was all wound neatly about him; clapped his cap on his head, very much on one side (for it could not stand upright without going through the ceiling), gave an additional twist to his corkscrew moustaches, and replied with perfect coolness: "Gentlemen, I wish you a very good morning. At twelve o'clock tonight I'll call again; after such a refusal of hospitality as I have just experienced, you will not be surprised if that visit is the last I ever pay you."

"If ever I catch you here again," muttered Schwartz, coming half frightened out of the corner—but, before he could finish his sentence, the old gentleman had shut the house door behind him with a great bang; and there drove past the window, at the same instant, a wreath of ragged cloud, that whirled and rolled away down the valley in all manner of shapes; turning over and over in the air; and melting away at last in a gush of rain.

"A very pretty business, indeed, Mr Gluck!" said Schwartz. "Dish the mutton, sir. If ever I catch you at such a trick again—bless me, why the mutton's been cut!"

"You promised me one slice, brother, you know," said Gluck.

"Oh! and you were cutting it hot, I suppose, and going to catch all the gravy. It'll be long before I promise you such a thing again. Leave the room, sir; and have the kindness to wait in the coal-cellar till I call you."

Gluck left the room, melancholy enough. The brothers ate as much mutton as they could, locked the rest in the cupboard, and proceeded to get very drunk after dinner.

Such a night it was! Howling wind and rushing rain, without intermission. The brothers had just sense enough left to put up all the shutters, and double bar the door, before they went to bed. They usually slept in the same room. As the clock struck twelve they were both awakened by a tremendous crash. Their door burst open with a violence that shook the house from top to bottom.

"What's that?" cried Schwartz, starting up in his bed.

"Only I," said the little gentleman.

The two brothers sat up on their bolster, and stared into the darkness. The room was full of water, and by a misty moonbeam, which found its way through a hole in the shutter, they could see in the midst of it an enormous foam globe, spinning round, and bobbing up and down like a cork, on which, as on a most luxurious cushion, reclined the little old gentleman, cap and all. There was plenty of room for it now, for the roof was off.

"Sorry to incommode you," said their visitor, ironically. "I'm afraid your beds are dampish; perhaps you had better go to your brother's room: I've left the ceiling on, there."

They required no second admonition, but rushed into Gluck's room, wet through, and in an agony of terror.

"You'll find my card on the kitchen table," the old gentleman called after them. "Remember, the *last* visit."

"Pray Heaven it may!" said Schwartz, shuddering. And the foam globe disappeared.

Dawn came at last, and the two brothers looked out of Gluck's little window in the morning. The Treasure Valley was one mass of ruin and desolation. The inundation had swept away trees, crops, and cattle, and left in their stead a waste of red sand and grey mud. The two brothers crept shivering and horror-struck into the kitchen. The water had gutted the whole first floor; corn, money, almost every movable thing, had been swept away, and there was left only a small white card on the kitchen table. On it, in large, breezy, long-legged letters, were engraved the words:

South West Wind, Esquire, was as good as his word. After the momentous visit above related, he entered the Treasure Valley no more; and, what was worse, he had so much influence with his relations, the West Winds in general, and used it so effectually, that they all adopted a similar line of conduct. So no rain fell in the valley from one year's end to another. Though everything remained green and flourishing in the plains below, the inheritance of the Three Brothers was a desert. What had once been the richest soil in the kingdom became a shifting heap of red sand; and the brothers, unable longer to contend with the adverse skies, abandoned their valueless patrimony in despair, to seek some means of gaining a livelihood among the cities and people of the plains. All their money was gone, and they had nothing left but some curious old-fashioned pieces of gold plate, the last remnants of their ill-gotten wealth.

"Suppose we turn goldsmiths?" said Schwartz to Hans, as they entered the large city. "It is a good knaves' trade; we can put a great deal of copper into the gold, without anyone's finding it out."

The thought was agreed to be a very good one; they hired a furnace, and turned goldsmiths. But two slight circumstances affected their trade: the first, that people did not approve of the coppered gold; the second, that the two elder brothers, whenever they had sold anything, used to leave little Gluck to mind the furnace and go and drink out the money in the ale-house next door. So they melted all their gold without making money enough to buy more, and were at last reduced to one large drinking-mug which an uncle of his had given to little Gluck, and which he was very fond of and would not have parted with for the world; though he never drank anything out of it but milk and water. The mug was a very odd mug to look at. The handle was formed of two wreaths of flowing golden hair, so finely spun that it looked more like silk than metal, and these wreaths descended into and mixed with a beard and whiskers, of the same exquisite workmanship, which surrounded and decorated a very fierce little face, of the reddest gold imaginable, right in the front of the mug, with a pair of eyes in it which seemed to command its whole circumference. It was impossible to drink out of the mug without being subjected to an intense gaze out of the side of these eyes; and Schwartz positively averred, that once, after emptying it, full of Rhenish, seventeen times, he had seen them wink! When it came to the mug's turn to be made into spoons, it half broke poor little Gluck's heart; but the brothers only laughed at him, tossed the mug into the melting-pot, and staggered out to the ale-house; leaving him, as usual, to pour the gold into bars, when it was all ready.

When they were gone, Gluck took a farewell look at his old friend in the melting-pot. The flowing hair was all gone; nothing remained but the red nose and the sparkling eyes, which looked

more malicious than ever. "And no wonder," thought Gluck, "after being treated in that way." He sauntered disconsolately to the window, and sat himself down to catch the fresh evening air, and escape the hot breath of the furnace. Now this window commanded a direct view of the range of mountains, which, as I told you before, overhung the Treasure Valley, and more especially of the peak from which fell the Golden River. It was just at the close of the day, and, when Gluck sat down at the window, he saw the rocks of the mountain tops, all crimson and purple with the sunset; and there were bright tongues of fiery cloud burning and quivering about them; and the river, brighter than all, fell, in a waving column of pure gold, from precipice to precipice, with the double arch of a broad purple rainbow stretched across it, flushing and fading alternately in the wreaths of spray.

"Ah!" said Gluck aloud, after he had looked at it for a little while, "if that river were really all gold, what a nice thing it would be."

"No it wouldn't, Gluck," said a clear, metallic voice close at his ear.

"Bless me, what's that?" exclaimed Gluck, jumping up. There was nobody there. He looked round the room, and under the table, and a great many times behind him, but there was certainly nobody there, and he sat down again at the window. This time he didn't speak, but he couldn't help thinking again that it would be very convenient if the river were really all gold.

"Not at all, my boy," said the same voice, louder than before.

"Bless me!" said Gluck again, "what *is* that?" He looked again into all the corners and cupboards, and then began turning round and round, as fast as he could, in the middle of the room, thinking there was somebody behind him, when the same voice struck again on his ear. It was singing now very merrily "Lala-lira-la"; no words, only a soft running effervescent melody, something like that of a kettle on the boil. Gluck looked out of the window. No, it was certainly in the house. Upstairs and downstairs. No, it was certainly in that very room, coming in quicker time, and clearer notes, every moment. "Lala-lira-la." All at once it struck Gluck that it sounded louder near the furnace. He ran to the opening, and looked in: yes, he was right, it seemed to be coming, not only out of the furnace, but out of the pot. He uncovered it, and ran back in a great fright, for the pot was certainly singing! He stood in the farthest corner of the room, with his hands up, and his mouth open, for a minute or two, when the singing stopped, and the voice became clear and pronunciative.

"Hallo!" said the voice.

Gluck made no answer.

"Hallo, Gluck, my boy!" said the pot again.

Gluck summoned all his energies, walked straight up to the crucible, drew it out of the furnace, and looked in. The gold was all melted, and its surface as smooth and polished as a river; but instead of reflecting little Gluck's head, as he looked in, he saw meeting his glance, from beneath the gold, the red nose and sharp eyes of his friend of the mug, a thousand times redder and sharper than ever he had seen them in his life.

"Come, Gluck, my boy," said the voice out of the pot again, "I'm all right; pour me out."

But Gluck was too much astonished to do anything of the kind.

"Pour me out, I say," said the voice rather gruffly.

Still Gluck couldn't move.

"*Will* you pour me out?" said the voice passionately; "I'm too hot."

By a violent effort, Gluck recovered the use of his limbs, took hold of the crucible, and sloped it, so as to pour out the gold. But instead of a liquid stream, there came out, first, a pair of pretty little yellow legs, then some coat-tails, then a pair of arms stuck a-kimbo, and, finally, the well-known

head of his friend the mug; all which articles, uniting as they rolled out, stood up energetically on the floor, in the shape of a little golden dwarf, about a foot and a half high.

"That's right!" said the dwarf, stretching out first his legs, and then his arms, and then shaking his head up and down, and as far round as it would go, for five minutes, without stopping; apparently with the view of ascertaining if he were quite correctly put together, while Gluck stood contemplating him in speechless amazement. He was dressed in a slashed doublet of spun gold, so fine in its texture that the prismatic colours gleamed over it, as if on a surface of mother-of-pearl; and, over this brilliant doublet, his hair and beard fell full half-way to the ground, in waving curls, so exquisitely delicate, that Gluck could hardly tell where they ended; they seemed to melt into air. The features of the face, however, were by no means finished with the same delicacy; they were rather coarse, slightly inclining to coppery in complexion, and indicative, in expression, of a very pertinacious and intractable disposition in their small proprietor. When the dwarf had finished his self-examination, he turned his small sharp eyes full on Gluck, and stared at him deliberately for a minute or two. "No it wouldn't, Gluck, my boy," said the little man.

This was certainly rather an abrupt and unconnected mode of commencing conversation. It might indeed be supposed to refer to the course of Gluck's thoughts, which had first produced the dwarf's observations out of the pot; but whatever it referred to, Gluck had no inclination to dispute the dictum.

"Wouldn't it, sir?" said Gluck, very mildly and submissively indeed.

"No," said the dwarf conclusively. "No, it wouldn't." And with that, the dwarf pulled his cap hard over his brows, and took two turns, of three feet long, up and down the room, lifting his legs up very high, and setting them down very hard. This pause gave time for Gluck to collect his thoughts a little; and, seeing no great reason to view his diminutive visitor with dread, and feeling his curiosity overcome his amazement, he ventured on a question of peculiar delicacy.

"Pray, sir," said Gluck rather hesitatingly, "were you my mug?"

On which the little man turned sharp round, walked straight up to Gluck, and drew himself up to his full height. "I," said the little man, "am the King of the Golden River." Whereupon he turned about again, and took two more turns, some six feet long, in order to allow time for the consternation which this announcement produced in his auditor to evaporate. After which, he again walked up to Gluck and stood still, as if expecting some comment on his communication.

Gluck determined to say something at all events. "I hope your majesty is very well," said Gluck.

"Listen!" said the little man, deigning no reply to this polite inquiry. "I am the King of what you mortals call the Golden River. The shape you saw me in was owing to the malice of a stronger king, from whose enchantments you have this instant freed me. What I have seen of you, and your conduct to your wicked brothers, renders me willing to serve you; therefore attend to what I tell you. Whoever shall climb to the top of that mountain from which you see the Golden River issue, and shall cast into the stream at its source three drops of holy water, for him, and for him only, the river shall turn to gold. But no one failing in his first, can succeed in a second attempt; and if anyone shall cast unholy water into the river, it will overwhelm him, and he will become a black stone." So saying, the King of the Golden River turned away, and deliberately walked into the centre of the hottest flame of the furnace. His figure became red, white, transparent, dazzling—a blaze of intense light—rose, trembled, and disappeared. The King of the Golden River had evaporated.

"Oh!" cried poor Gluck, running to look up the chimney after him. "Oh dear, dear, dear me! My mug! My mug! My mug!"

The King of the Golden River had hardly made the extraordinary exit related in the last chapter before Hans and Schwartz came roaring into the house, very savagely drunk. The discovery of the total loss of their last piece of plate had the effect of sobering them just enough to enable them to stand over Gluck, beating him very steadily for a quarter of an hour; at the expiration of which period they dropped into a couple of chairs, and requested to know what he had got to say for himself. Gluck told them his story, of which of course they did not believe a word. They beat him again, till their arms were tired, and staggered to bed. In the morning, however, the steadiness with which he adhered to his story obtained him some degree of credence; the immediate consequence of which was, that the two brothers, after wrangling a long time on the knotty question, which of them should try his fortune first, drew their swords and began fighting. The noise of the fray alarmed the neighbours, who, finding they could not pacify the combatants, sent for the constable.

Hans, on hearing this, contrived to escape, and hid himself; but Schwartz was taken before the magistrate, fined for breaking the peace, and, having drunk out his last penny the evening before, was thrown into prison till he should pay.

When Hans heard this, he was much delighted, and determined to set out immediately for the Golden River. How to get the holy water, was the question. He went to the priest, but the priest could not give any holy water to so abandoned a character. So Hans went to vespers in the evening for the first time in his life, and, under pretence of crossing himself, stole a cupful, and returned home in triumph.

Next morning he got up before the sun rose, put the holy water into a strong flask, and two bottles of wine and some meat in a basket, slung them over his back, took his alpine staff in his hand, and set off for the mountains.

On his way out of the town, he had to pass the prison, and as he looked in at the windows, whom should he see but Schwartz himself peeping out of the bars, and looking very disconsolate.

"Good morning, brother," said Hans; "have you any message for the King of the Golden River?"

Schwartz gnashed his teeth with rage, and shook the bars with all his strength; but Hans only laughed at him, and, advising him to make himself comfortable till he came back again, shouldering his basket, shook the bottle of holy water in Schwartz's face till it frothed again, and marched off in the highest spirits in the world.

It was, indeed, a morning that might have made anyone happy, even with no Golden River to seek for. Level lines of dewy mist lay stretched along the valley, out of which rose the massy mountains—their lower cliffs in pale grey shadow, hardly distinguishable from the floating vapour, but gradually ascending till they caught the sunlight, which ran in sharp touches of ruddy colour along the angular crags, and pierced, in long level rays, through their fringes of spear-like pine. Far above, shot up red splintered masses of castellated rock, jagged and shivered into myriads of fantastic forms, with here and there a streak of sunlit snow, traced down their chasms like a line of forked lightning; and, far beyond, and far above all these, fainter than the morning cloud, but purer and changeless, slept, in the blue sky, the utmost peaks of the eternal snow.

The Golden River, which sprang from one of the lower and snowless elevations, was now nearly in shadow; all but the uppermost jets of spray, which rose like slow smoke above the undulating line of the cataract, and floated away in feeble wreaths upon the morning wind.

On this object, and on this alone, Hans's eyes and thoughts were fixed; forgetting the distance he had to traverse, he set off at an imprudent rate of walking, which greatly exhausted him before he had scaled the first range of the green and low hills. He was, moreover, surprised, on surmounting them, to find that a large glacier, of whose existence, notwithstanding his previous knowledge of the mountains, he had been absolutely ignorant, lay between him and the source of the Golden River. He entered on it with the boldness of a practised mountaineer; yet he thought he had never traversed so strange or so dangerous a glacier in his life.

The ice was excessively slippery, and out of all its chasms came wild sounds of gushing water; not monotonous or low, but changeful and loud, rising occasionally into drifting passages of wild melody, then breaking off into short, melancholy tones, or sudden shrieks, resembling those of human voices in distress or pain.

The ice was broken into thousands of confused shapes, but none, Hans thought, like the ordinary forms of splintered ice. There seemed a curious *expression* about all their outlines—a perpetual resemblance to living features, distorted and scornful. Myriads of deceitful shadows, and lurid lights, played and floated about and through the pale blue pinnacles, dazzling and confusing the sight of the traveller; while his ears grew dull and his head giddy with the constant gush and roar of the concealed waters. These painful circumstances increased upon him as he advanced; the ice crashed and yawned into fresh chasms at his feet, tottering spires nodded around him, and fell thundering across his path; and though he had repeatedly faced these dangers on the most terrific glaciers, and in the wildest weather, it was with a new and oppressive feeling of panic terror that he leaped the last chasm, and flung himself, exhausted and shuddering, on the firm turf of the mountain.

He had been compelled to abandon his basket of food, which became a perilous encumbrance on the glacier, and had now no means of refreshing himself but by breaking off and eating some of the pieces of ice. This, however, relieved his thirst; an hour's repose recruited his hardy frame, and, with the indomitable spirit of avarice, he resumed his laborious journey.

His way now lay straight up a ridge of bare red rocks, without a blade of grass to ease the foot, or a projecting angle to afford an inch of shade from the south sun. It was past noon, and the rays beat intensely upon the steep path, while the whole atmosphere was motionless, and penetrated with heat. Intense thirst was soon added to the bodily fatigue with which Hans was now afflicted; glance after glance he cast on the flask of water which hung at his belt. "Three drops are enough," at last thought he; "I may, at least, cool my lips with it."

He opened the flask, and was raising it to his lips, when his eye fell on an object lying on the rock beside him; he thought it moved. It was a small dog, apparently in the last agony of death from thirst. Its tongue was out, its jaws dry, its limbs extended lifelessly, and a swarm of black ants were crawling about its lips and throat. Its eye moved to the bottle which Hans held in his hand. He raised it, drank, spurned the animal with his foot, and passed on. And he did not know how it was, but he thought that a strange shadow had suddenly come across the blue sky.

The path became steeper and more rugged every moment; and the high hill air, instead of refreshing him, seemed to throw his blood into a fever. The noise of the hill cataracts sounded like mockery in his ears: they were all distant, and his thirst increased every moment. Another hour passed, and he again looked down to the flask at his side; it was half empty, but there was much more than three drops in it. He stopped to open it, and again, as he did so, something moved in the path above him. It was a fair child, stretched nearly lifeless on the rock, its breast heaving with thirst, its eyes closed, and its lips parched and burning. Hans eyed it deliberately, drank, and passed on. And a dark grey cloud came over the sun, and long, snake-like shadows crept up along the mountainsides. Hans struggled on. The sun was sinking, but its descent seemed to bring no coolness; the leaden weight of the dead air pressed upon his brow and heart, but the goal was near. He saw the cataract of the Golden River springing from the hillside, scarcely five hundred feet above him. He paused for a moment to breathe, and sprang on to complete his task.

At this instant a faint cry fell on his ear. He turned, and saw a grey-haired old man extended on the rocks. His eyes were sunk, his features deadly pale, and gathered into an expression of despair. "Water!" He stretched his arms to Hans, and cried feebly: "Water! I am dying."

"I have none," replied Hans; "thou hast had thy share of life." He strode over the prostrate body and darted on. And a flash of blue lightning rose out of the East, shaped like a sword; it shook thrice over the whole heaven, and left it dark with one heavy, impenetrable shade. The sun was setting; it plunged towards the horizon like a red-hot ball.

The roar of the Golden River rose on Hans's ear. He stood at the brink of the chasm through which it ran. Its waves were filled with the red glory of the sunset; they shook their crests like tongues of fire, and flashes of blood-red light gleamed along their foam. Their sound came mightier and mightier on his senses; his brain grew giddy with the prolonged thunder. Shuddering, he drew the flask from his girdle and hurled it into the centre of the torrent. As he did so, an icy chill shot through his limbs; he staggered, shrieked, and fell. The waters closed over his cry. And the moaning of the river rose wildly into the night, as it gushed over **The Black Stone.**

Poor little Gluck waited very anxiously alone in the house for Hans's return. Finding he did not come back, he was terribly frightened, and went and told Schwartz in the prison all that had happened. Then Schwartz was very much pleased, and said that Hans must certainly have been turned into a black stone, and he should have all the gold to himself. But Gluck was very sorry and cried all night. When he got up in the morning there was no bread in the house, nor any money; so Gluck went and hired himself to another goldsmith, and he worked so hard, and so neatly, and so long every day, that he soon got money enough together to pay his brother's fine, and he went and gave it all to Schwartz, and Schwartz got out of prison. Then Schwartz was quite pleased, and said he should have some of the gold of the river. But Gluck only begged he would go and see what had become of Hans.

Now when Schwartz had heard that Hans had stolen the holy water, he thought to himself that such a proceeding might not be considered altogether correct by the King of the Golden River, and determined to manage matters better. So he took some more of Gluck's money, and went to a bad priest, who gave him some holy water very readily for it. Then Schwartz was sure it was all quite right. So Schwartz got up early in the morning before the sun rose, and took some bread and wine in a basket, and put his holy water in a flask, and set off for the mountains. Like his brother he was much surprised at the sight of the glacier, and had great difficulty in crossing it, even after leaving his basket behind him. The day was cloudless, but not bright: there was a heavy purple haze hanging

over the sky, and the hills looked lowering and gloomy. And as Schwartz climbed the steep rock path, the thirst came upon him, as it had upon his brother, until he lifted his flask to his lips to drink. Then he saw the fair child lying near him on the rocks, and it cried to him, and moaned for water.

"Water, indeed," said Schwartz; "I haven't half enough for myself," and passed on. And as he went he thought the sunbeams grew more dim, and he saw a low bank of black cloud rising out of the west; and, when he had climbed for another hour, the thirst overcame him again, and he would have drunk. Then he saw the old man lying before him on the path, and heard him cry out for water.

"Water, indeed," said Schwartz; "I haven't half enough for myself," and on he went.

Then again the light seemed to fade from before his eyes, and he looked up, and, behold, a mist, of the colour of blood, had come over the sun; and the bank of black cloud had risen very high, and its edges were tossing and tumbling like the waves of the angry sea. And they cast long shadows, which flickered over Schwartz's path.

Then Schwartz climbed for another hour, and again his thirst returned; and as he lifted his flask to his lips, he thought he saw his brother Hans lying exhausted on the path before him, and, as he gazed, the figure stretched its arms to him, and cried for water. "Ha, ha," laughed Schwartz, "are you there? Remember the prison bars, my boy. Water, indeed! Do you suppose I carried it all the way up here for *you*?" And he strode over the figure; yet, as he passed, he thought he saw a strange expression of mockery about its lips. And, when he had gone a few yards farther, he looked back; but the figure was not there.

And a sudden horror came over Schwartz, he knew not why; but the thirst for gold prevailed over his fear, and he rushed on. And the bank of black cloud rose to the zenith, and out of it came bursts of spiry lightning, and waves of darkness seemed to heave and float, between their flashes, over the whole heavens. And the sky where the sun was setting was all level, and like a lake of blood; and a strong wind came out of that sky, tearing its crimson clouds into fragments, and scattering them far into the darkness. And when Schwartz stood by the brink of the Golden River, its waves were black, like thunder clouds, but their foam was like fire; and the roar of the waters below and the thunder above met, as he cast the flask into the stream. And, as he did so, the lightning glared in his eyes, and the earth gave way beneath him, and the waters closed over his cry. And the moaning of the river rose wildly into the night, as it gushed over **The Two Black Stones.**

When Gluck found that Schwartz did not come back, he was very sorry, and did not know what to do. He had no money, and was obliged to go and hire himself again to the goldsmith, who worked him very hard, and gave him very little money. So, after a month or two, Gluck grew tired, and made up his mind to go and try his fortune with the Golden River. "The little King looked very kind," thought he. "I don't think he will turn me into a black stone." So he went to the priest, and the priest gave him some holy water as soon as he asked for it. Then Gluck took some bread in his basket, and the bottle of water, and set off very early for the mountains.

If the glacier had occasioned a great deal of fatigue to his brothers, it was twenty times worse for him, who was neither so strong nor so practised on the mountains. He had several very bad falls, lost his basket and bread, and was very much frightened at the strange noises under the ice. He lay a long time to rest on the grass, after he had got over, and began to climb the hill just in the hottest part of the day. When he had climbed for an hour he got dreadfully thirsty, and was going to drink like his brothers, when he saw an old man coming down the path above him, looking very feeble, and leaning on a staff. "My son," said the old man, "I am faint with thirst—give me some of that water." Then Gluck looked at him, and when he saw that he was pale and weary, he gave him the water: "Only pray don't drink it all," said Gluck. But the old man drank a great deal, and gave him back the bottle two-thirds empty. Then he bade him good speed, and Gluck went on again merrily. And the path became easier to his feet, and two or three blades of grass appeared upon it, and some grasshoppers began singing on the bank beside it; and Gluck thought he had never heard such merry singing.

Then he went on for another hour, and the thirst increased on him so that he thought he should be forced to drink. But, as he raised the flask, he saw a little child lying panting by the roadside, and it cried out piteously for water. Then Gluck struggled with himself, and determined to bear the thirst a little longer; and he put the bottle to the child's lips, and it drank it all but a few drops. Then it smiled on him, and got up, and ran down the hill; and Gluck looked after it, till it became as small as a little star, and then turned, and began climbing again. And then there were all kinds of sweet flowers growing on the rocks, bright green moss, with pale pink starry flowers, and soft-belled gentians, more blue than the sky at its deepest, and pure white transparent lilies. And crimson and purple butterflies darted hither and thither, and the sky sent down such pure light that Gluck had never felt so happy in his life.

Yet, when he had climbed for another hour, his thirst became intolerable again; and, when he looked at his bottle, he saw that there were only five or six drops left in it, and he could not venture to drink. And, as he was hanging the flask to his belt again, he saw a little dog lying on the rocks, gasping for breath—just as Hans had seen it on the day of his ascent. And Gluck stopped and looked at it, and then at the Golden River, not five hundred yards above him; and he thought of the dwarf's words, "that no one could succeed, except in their first attempt"; and he tried to pass the dog, but it whined piteously, and Gluck stopped again. "Poor beastie," said Gluck, "it'll be dead when I come down again, if I don't help it." Then he looked closer and closer at it, and its eye turned on him so mournfully that he could not stand it. "Confound the King and his gold too," said Gluck; and he opened the flask and poured all the water into the dog's mouth.

The dog sprang up and stood on its hind legs. Its tail disappeared, its ears became long, longer, silky, golden; its nose became very red, its eyes became very twinkling; in three seconds the dog was gone, and before Gluck stood his old acquaintance, the King of the Golden River.

"Thank you," said the monarch, "but don't be frightened, it's all right"; for Gluck showed manifest symptoms of consternation at this unlooked-for reply to his last observation. "Why didn't you come before," continued the dwarf, "instead of sending me those rascally brothers of yours, for me to have the trouble of turning into stones? Very hard stones they make too."

"Oh dear me!" said Gluck. "Have you really been so cruel?"

"Cruel!" said the dwarf. "They poured unholy water into my stream: do you suppose I'm going to allow that?"

"Why," said Gluck, "I am sure, sir—your majesty, I mean—they got the water out of the church font."

"Very probably," replied the dwarf; "but"—and his countenance grew stern as he spoke—"the water which has been refused to the cry of the weary and dying is unholy, though it has been blessed by every saint in heaven; and the water which is found in the vessel of mercy is holy, though it had been defiled with corpses."

So saying, the dwarf stooped and plucked a lily that grew at his feet. On its white leaves there hung three drops of clear dew. And the dwarf shook them into the flask which Gluck held in his hand. "Cast these into the river," he said, "and descend on the other side of the mountains into the Treasure Valley. And so good speed."

As he spoke, the figure of the dwarf became indistinct. The playing colours of his robe formed themselves into a prismatic mist of dewy light: he stood for an instant veiled with them as with the belt of a broad rainbow. The colours grew faint, the mist rose into the air; the monarch had evaporated.

And Gluck climbed to the brink of the Golden River, and its waves were as clear as crystal, and as brilliant as the sun. And, when he cast the three drops of dew into the stream, there opened where they fell a small circular whirlpool, into which the waters descended with a musical noise. Gluck stood watching it for some time, very much disappointed, because not only was the river not turned into gold, but its waters seemed much diminished in quantity. Yet he obeyed his friend the dwarf, and descended the other side of the mountains, towards the Treasure Valley; and, as he went, he thought he heard the noise of water working its way under the ground. And, when he came in sight of the Treasure Valley, behold, a river, like the Golden River, was springing from a new cleft of the rocks above it, and was flowing in innumerable streams among the dry heaps of red sand. And as Gluck gazed, fresh grass sprang beside the new streams, and creeping plants grew, and climbed among the moistening soil. Young flowers opened suddenly along the riversides, as stars leap out when twilight is deepening, and thickets of myrtle, and tendrils of vine, cast lengthening shadows over the valley as they grew.

And thus the Treasure Valley became a garden again, and the inheritance, which had been lost by cruelty, was regained by love. And Gluck went and dwelt in the valley, and the poor were never driven from his door; so that his barns became full of corn, and his house of treasure. And for him the river had, according to the dwarf's promise, become a River of Gold. And to this day the inhabitants of the valley point to the place where the three drops of holy dew were cast into the stream, and trace the course of the Golden River under the ground, until it emerges in the Treasure Valley. And at the top of the cataract of the Golden River are still to be seen two Black Stones, round which the waters howl mournfully every day at sunset; and these stones are still called by the people of the valley, **The Black Brothers.**